'Ouch!' gasped Max. He felt his cheeks bubble and wriggle, as if he was making faces at Molly. His mouth grew wide in a big grin, and the back of his neck hurt like mad as a fold of skin sprouted out like a little cape. His ribs seemed to push outwards and flatten sideways as if someone had sat on him rather hard. His bottom hurt too. The base of his spine seemed to unfold and stretch, then curl itself round into a spring. His elbows shrieked with pain as his arms shrank into his body and something very weird started happening to his feet. He tried to move, feeling his fingers and toes grapple something. They'd kind of fused, so that he had three digits stuck together on one side and two on the other.

He felt as if he was going to fall over, but his tail coiled itself grimly round something hard. Then, suddenly, everything went dark.

One school holiday, Max and Molly go with their zoologist parents to Africa. Max develops a strange fever when he drinks from a stream and, after he's recovered, everything has changed – especially his attitude to animals.

The village healer tells him he now has a special skill: he's at one with the animals. But Max doesn't believe a word of it. At least, not until the first time his fingers tingle, his vision goes wobbly and his tongue gets thick and fuzzy . . .

Luckily, the effects never last more than a few hours, but that's still plenty of time for Max to get into some amazing scrapes, and to get first-hand experience of how the animal world sees humans.

For a boy who wants nothing more challenging than a computer game and a chocolate bar, life just got a whole lot more complicated . . .

BEASTLY!

CHAMELEON CRISIS

Andy Baxter

Illustrations by Brian Williamson

EGMONT

Special thanks to:
Ann Ruffell, West Jesmond Primary School,
Maney Hill Primary School
and Courthouse Junior School

EGMONT
We bring stories to life

Chameleon Crisis first published in Great Britain 2008
by Egmont UK Limited
239 Kensington High Street, London W8 6SA

Text & illustrations © 2008 Egmont UK Ltd
Text by Ann Ruffell
Illustrations by Brian Williamson

ISBN 978 1 4052 3940 0

1 3 5 7 9 10 8 6 4 2

A CIP catalogue record for this title is available
from the British Library

Typeset by Avon DataSet Ltd, Bidford on Avon, Warwickshire
Printed and bound in Great Britain by the CPI Group

MAX MURPHY Fast-food
fan who just can't help
ordering extra *flies*

Absent-minded Uncle Herbert looks after
Max and his twin sister Molly during term
time while their parents are away.

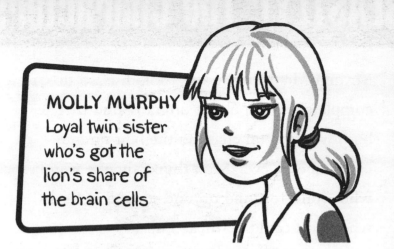

MOLLY MURPHY
Loyal twin sister who's got the lion's share of the brain cells

Max longs for a normal family life, but that's about as likely as his uncle remembering which day of the week it is!

HERBERT SPLOTT
Wacky uncle with a weird set of taste buds

BEASTLY!: The Characters

Mr and Mrs Murphy are zoologists, so they're completely crazy about animals, and they're busy working on creating the best animal encyclopedia ever. Max thinks they're weird; who wants to stand around staring at sloths when you could be tucked up at home watching telly?

MR MURPHY AND MRS MURPHY
Can't see the truth about their son ... but then again he is camouflaged!

PROFESSOR SLYNK
You don't need a heightened sense of smell to catch a whiff of this crook

And, as if all that didn't make Max's life tough enough, his parents' sinister colleague Professor Preston Slynk has found out his secret. Slynk's miniature insect-robot spies are never far away . . .

CHAMELEONS:

They're changeable!
Contrary to popular belief, a chameleon doesn't usually change colour to match its surroundings. Instead, colour is usually used to show emotions, defend territories, and communicate with other chameleons.

They love Madagascar!
Over 70 per cent of the world's chameleon population live on the island of Madagascar.

They're lions!
Well, sort of. The word chameleon means 'earth lion' and comes from two Greek words – *chamai* (on the earth) and *leon* (lion).

The Facts

They can be weeny!
The smallest chameleon is a mere 2.5 centimetres in length!

They can be huge!
The biggest chameleon measures 79 centimetres. (Yikes – it's a dinosaur!)

They have the weirdest eyes!
Each eye can move and focus separately, which gives them 360-degree vision and the ability to look at two things at once!

MADAGASCAR:

- Its population is around 18 million
- It was once joined on to Africa but about 160 million years ago, it separated to become an island
- It's about the size of France. And that's not the only thing the two countries have in common – French is spoken by many educated in Madagascar

ARCTIC OCEAN

North America

ATLANTIC OCEAN

Eur

South America

PACIFIC OCEAN

ATLANTIC OCEAN

SOUTHERN OCEAN

The Facts

- It has two seasons: a hot, rainy season from November to April and a cooler, dry season from May to October
- About 75 per cent of the species found in Madagascar live nowhere else on the planet!

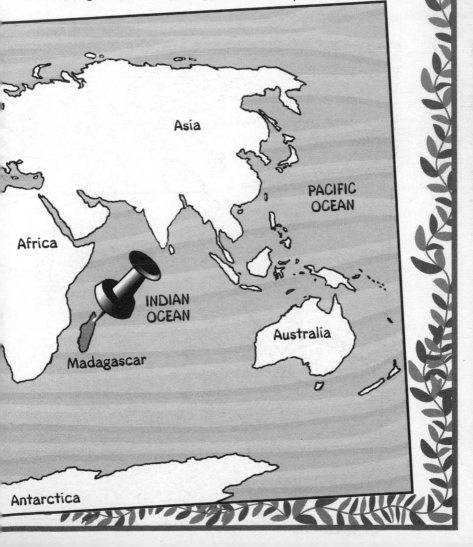

Contents

1. Madagascan Misery

'How many times do you think I can get this to skip?' asked Molly, as she held up a smooth, flat stone.

'Dunno,' shrugged Max. 'Once?'

'Once?!' his twin sister shrilled. 'I could do it once in my sleep!'

Max leant back on the rock he was sitting on and squinted in the midday sun. He shuffled a little to the left so Molly's shadow blocked out the glare.

'Twice then,' he sighed.

'Ten times – easy,' Molly crowed, as she turned to face the vast, motionless lake which lay before them. 'Or I'll be your slave for the day.'

'I'm not being *your* slave if you do it though,' Max quickly insisted.

'That's OK,' his sister shrugged, 'you're more or less my slave anyway.'

Molly closed one eye, held her breath, and flicked the stone out over the water. It skimmed the surface a dozen times before sinking below the brilliant blue surface.

'Twelve times!' she beamed.

'You must be very proud,' said Max, sarcastically.

'Now then,' Molly began, 'how many times do you think I can skip *this* one?'

Max placed his hands behind his head and lay back on the rock. He closed his eyes and did his best to block out Molly's chattering. Even with his

2

eyes closed he could still see the bright orange tones of the blazing sun.

Of all the terrible trips their parents had brought them on, this was one of the worst. He knew, of course, that his mum and dad wouldn't go anywhere if there weren't a wide range of animals to study, but he hadn't expected Madagascar to be quite so full of the things.

On their first day on the island their dad had told them that 5 per cent of the world's animal species could be found in Madagascar. By the end of the fourth day Max felt like he'd changed into almost all of them. At the last count he'd been a longhorn beetle, a praying mantis, a fork-crowned lemur and a tomato frog. Apart from the praying mantis, he'd never even heard of any of them before this trip! His transformations often turned into really exciting adventures, but with so many changes — well, it was just too much.

'You'd better not fall asleep, you'll get sunstroke,' Molly warned him.

'I'm tired,' Max groaned. 'It's not easy changing every few hours!'

'*You're* tired?' his sister snapped. 'I'm the one who has to trudge around trying to find you whenever you transform. Have you any idea how hard it is to find one little red frog in a rainforest?'

'Have you any idea how hard it is to *be* one little red frog in a rainforest?' Max replied. He sat up on the rock and shielded his eyes with his hand. 'There are things in there that eat little red frogs for breakfast.' Just then his stomach gave a loud rumble. 'Speaking of which, it's lunchtime.'

'Do you ever think about anything apart from food?'

'Course,' sniffed Max, as he got to his feet and dusted himself down. 'If I'm not hungry I don't think about food at all.'

'Oh, yeah? And when are you not hungry?'

'Never!' Max grinned.

The twins walked slowly towards their hotel, dragging their feet behind them. Neither one was looking forward to another encounter with their parents, who had been cross with them for almost the entire trip.

'You think Mum and Dad are still annoyed?' Max asked.

'Probably,' Molly replied. 'They still think we've spent the week sleeping and hanging around the hotel. I bet they had lots of educational day trips planned for us.'

'You know, when you put it like that,' said Max, 'being chased by hungry snakes yesterday suddenly doesn't seem quite so bad.'

'D'you think we should tell them the truth?'

Max stopped and stared at his sister.

'Are you crazy?' he gasped. 'I thought we agreed never to tell them?'

'I know, I just thought it might make life easier,' Molly suggested. 'Instead of having to hide things all the time.'

'I wouldn't be able to hide anything even if I wanted to. They wouldn't let me out of their sight! They'd have a book written all about me in a week, and I could wave goodbye to any chance of a normal life!'

Molly shrugged as they started walking again.
'Yeah, I suppose.'

'So we keep it to ourselves, right?'

'Right,' Molly nodded.

They shuffled on in silence for a few minutes, each lost in their own thoughts.

'D'you think anyone's found those jewels yet?' asked Molly, eventually.

'Which jewels?'

'The stolen jewels,' said Molly. Max looked at her, his face blank. 'The ones I've told you about four times now.' She sighed and shook her head. 'Do you ever listen to anything I say?'

'Sorry, did you say something?' smirked Max. 'I wasn't listening.'

Molly growled and punched her brother hard on the arm.

'There was a big shipment of diamonds and stuff being taken from Kuala Lumpur to Zambia for some prince or other,' she explained for the fifth time. 'It went missing when it was passing through here. I told you all this!'

'No, you didn't,' Max protested.

'I did too! *Four* times! Last time you said "Ooh, that's interesting" and then started talking about food.'

'Did I?' frowned Max. 'Interesting.' He lifted his nose in the air and smiled broadly. 'Now come on, I smell lunch!'

As the twins entered the hotel, Molly held up a hand for Max to stop. She put her finger to her lips and nodded in the direction of the hotel reception. Max looked over and felt his heart leap into his throat.

'Professor Sly-ink,' smiled the receptionist,

reading the name from the reservations book.

The overweight man in front of her mopped his sweaty brow with a spotty handkerchief and scowled. With his other hand he swatted wildly at the flies that buzzed around him.

'Slynk,' he corrected. 'Professor Preston Slynk.'

'Sly-ink,' said the receptionist, uncertainly.

'No, not Sly-ink. *Slynk.*'

'Ah! Slynk. Like stink?'

'Yes,' Slynk sighed. 'That's me.'

Molly let out a giggle and the twins had to duck behind a statue to avoid being seen by the professor.

'What's he doing here?' hissed Max, quietly.

'Mum said he might be coming,' Molly whispered.

'Why didn't you tell me?'

'I did!'

'Oh,' said Max. 'Well, why's he here?'

'Something to do with a night-vision telescope for watching lemurs,' Molly told him.

'I bet that's not the real reason,' said Max, grimly. 'He'll be after me the first chance he gets.'

'Maybe not,' Molly shrugged. 'Maybe he's really just here to help build the telescope. Or maybe,' she grinned, 'he's the one who stole the jewels and he's hanging around until he can get them out of the country.'

'Yeah,' Max laughed. 'He'll have used his little robot spies to do all the dirty work. No security system in the world could hope to stand in the way of Professor Preston Slynk, the greatest criminal mind of our time!'

'Maybe that's why his belly's so big,' added Molly. 'That's where he keeps all the stuff he steals!'

The twins fell about laughing, trying unsuccessfully to imagine Slynk as an international jewel thief.

'Maybe we should tell the police,' suggested Molly. 'It would be nice to see him slung into an African jail.'

'It would,' nodded Max, smiling at the thought. 'And I'd happily be the one to throw away the key!'

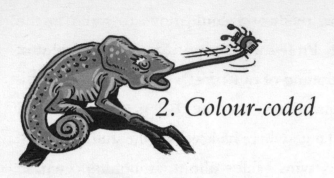

2. Colour-coded

Slynk was talking to a couple of local men in the hotel lobby as the lift arrived. He waved them away, then stepped inside.

The doors closed on Slynk and his luggage, and the twins sighed with relief.

'C'mon outside,' said Max. He looked nervously round the lobby. There didn't seem to be any animals, large or small, lurking there, but you never knew. If he was going to change into anything, he'd prefer to do it outside where the professor couldn't see him.

What he wanted more than anything else at this moment was to sit down quietly in front of his computer console and try to get through that tricky gate in his new *Jungle Juice* game, with a couple of bags of crisps to help him concentrate. At least then if he got eaten he only lost points.

'Where are Mum and Dad?' asked Molly. 'We don't want to bump into them either.'

'It's OK, they've gone out for a walk,' mumbled Max. He sighed. He'd remembered to bring the DVD, but his console was at home. Here in the Madagascar Hotel they didn't seem to have heard of computer games. And Mum wouldn't be too keen on him playing even if they had. But at least they'd gone out without dragging their children along to experience the lovely wildlife of Madagascar. Max shuddered. As if he didn't have enough experience of wildlife!

'Don't worry,' said Molly sympathetically. 'I'll make sure you're OK.'

'I tell you one thing for certain,' said Max, 'I'm not going out at night if Professor Stink's going to be lurking with his telescope!'

He tramped behind Molly, who was waving a fan of leaves in front of her face, though there didn't seem as many flies out here.

'What's that?' cried Molly, waving her leaf at a clump of trees.

'A tree, dork,' growled Max.

'Dork yourself. It's a whole *load* of trees, actually,' retorted Molly. She ran over to them. 'I meant, what was that noise?'

Max listened for lions roaring, or monkeys chattering. 'I don't know,' he said.

'There *is* something,' shrieked Molly, 'I can hear it!'

'Well, shut up, or it'll run away,' said Max.

14

Molly wasn't listening. She was peering amongst the leaves, pulling them apart to find whatever it was that was rustling. 'I can see something moving,' she shrilled, 'but I can't tell what!'

Max went over, curious to see for himself. Leaves shifted as if something invisible was walking all over them. 'Hang on,' he shouted, 'I can see something now!'

At first it looked like a leaf. But the strange, narrow body belonged to a chameleon; a little lizard with a tail as whirly as a snail shell and funny hooked feet. Its skin was mostly green with splodgy bits of pattern, like a picture where the paint has run. It clung grimly to its branch, its skin changing colour in panic.

'Oh, look,' said Molly. 'Isn't it sweet! It was exactly the colour of that leaf, but now it's going yellow. How do you think it does that? Aren't they supposed to change to fit in with the background? Well, this one hasn't. Do you think it doesn't know how to?'

Max tried to speak, but his mouth suddenly seemed full of tongue. And something very strange was happening to the tree. It had started growing, zooming up into the sky, taking most of its leaves with it. What had seemed to be a smooth trunk was now folded and dented like tractor tracks in a muddy field. And the lower leaves were growing too, spreading out right in front of his eyes. He could see every vein, every little hair, every . . . ant! They were enormous! One of the ants glared at him, but when Max opened his mouth it scurried off to join the rest of its mates down the rutted trunk.

His skin and scalp began to prickle as tiny cells changed into scales over his back and head. His back ached as it bent over like a bow.

'Ouch!' gasped Max as his backbone began popping spines through the scales. He could feel his cheeks bubble and wriggle, as if he was making faces at Molly. His mouth grew wide in a big grin, and the back of his neck hurt like mad as a fold of skin sprouted out like a little cape. His ribs seemed to push outwards and flatten sideways as if someone had sat on him rather hard. His bottom hurt too. The base of his spine seemed to unfold and stretch, then curl itself round into a spring. His elbows shrieked with pain as his arms shrank into his body and something very weird started happening to his feet. He tried to move, feeling his fingers and toes grapple something. They'd kind of fused, so that he had three digits stuck together on one side and two on the other.

He felt as if he was going to fall over, but his tail coiled itself grimly round something hard. Then, suddenly, everything went dark.

He thought there must be something wrong with his eyes. The lids had joined together and though he could swivel his eyeballs around he couldn't see.

He was really very worried about this. Then, as his claws moved slowly to the end of the thing they were gripping, brilliant sunlight suddenly shone into his eyes and he realised he was clutching the back of his trainers, peeping out of the end of his own crumpled trousers.

He swivelled one eye. *Hey, this is fantastic!* he thought to himself. He could see right behind him without having to move his head at all; there was his tail, coiled tightly round his belt. He experimented with the other eye, and it swivelled in the other direction, watching Molly, still chatting away about the chameleon on the branch. In fact, he seemed to be able to see things he normally couldn't see at all. Surely that flower hadn't had stripey bits inside when he'd looked five minutes ago? Or was it just because he didn't know his flowers very well?

Just as he was pondering this, Molly turned. 'What do you think Max? Oh, where have you gone?'

There was panic in her voice until she saw the T-shirt and trousers lying empty on the ground. 'Max? Max — what have you turned into now?' She lifted the clothes and shook them.

Hey, don't do that! Max felt his skin tingle. Hastily, he uncoiled his tail and dropped back into his shoe.

'Another chameleon! Is that you, Max? It's got to be — yes, you've got blue eyes! You've turned yellow too — are you frightened or something?'

He managed to crawl out of the shoe, then felt quite sick as Molly lifted him swiftly into the air and cuddled him. His skin felt hot, rather like when he blushed with embarrassment when Mum told strangers how wonderful he was. Molly watched him change colour, into stripes that matched her T-shirt perfectly.

Molly giggled. 'Brilliant! How did you do that?' She put him down on the ground and stood her tartan bag beside him. 'Can you change into that?'

Max swaggered over to the tartan bag and almost immediately became tartan.

Molly roared with laughter. 'That is so cool! Wait a minute – try this.' She took her sunglasses out of the bag and watched as Max waddled over them, clutching on to the arms of them with his little clawed feet. His skin changed into two great, dark lenses.

'*Amazing!*' she breathed. 'What else can you do? Hey, try this.' She pulled off the red-and-white spotted scarf that her mother insisted she wore to keep the sun off her neck. Obligingly, Max crept

over the scarf and disappeared into the spots.

'I'll just run back to the hotel and see what else I can find,' she chortled. 'Don't worry, I won't take you anywhere near Professor Stink.'

She turned. Her parents were standing behind her, their mouths agape.

She felt as if her heart had dropped right down into her trainers. How long had they been there? What had they seen?

3. A Lively Picnic

'Oh, hi,' gulped Molly. 'Had a nice walk?' She tried to pick Max up with the scarf, but her father got there first.

'What an amazing creature!' Mr Murphy lifted the chameleon up, and Max had that nasty sick feeling again. *I'll never pick up animals again*, he swore. He could feel his skin turning yellow.

'Now that's a much more normal reaction,' said Mrs Murphy, peering down at Max. 'People think chameleons change colour to blend into the background, but that simply isn't true.' She looked at Max doubtfully. 'That is, nobody has ever seen one that does what this one seems to be doing. They change colour to tell other chameleons what mood they're in – like yellow if they're frightened, or black when they're angry.'

'Interesting little chap,' said Mr Murphy. 'You see, Molly, they change with a combination of mood, light and temperature. And yet . . .' He looked at Max with a gleam of scientific curiosity in his eye. 'A new species, perhaps? It would be wonderful if we could show that this was the first chameleon to really do what people always think chameleons do!'

Molly gulped. They'd always been scared in case anyone took Max apart to see how his transformations happened. That was exactly what Professor Slynk wanted to do, but it would be just as bad if his parents took him apart to see how he changed colour!

'Look at its lovely blue eyes!' cooed Mrs Murphy, stroking Max's knobbly back.

'We must find out if it's the only one,' said Mr Murphy with determination. He scooped Max up in his hands and turned to Molly. 'We need to show this fellow to an expert as soon as possible. We have a friend . . .'

'You mean Sylvain?' said Mrs Murphy breathlessly. 'Of course! The perfect person. He's an expert on chameleons,' she told Molly. 'He lives in the capital – Antananarivo. He'll know whether there are other chameleons like this.'

'But . . .' began Molly.

'Yes, but we must hurry!' interrupted her father, frowning. 'He's in Antananarivo now, but he's going to Sri Lanka tomorrow, remember? And then he won't be back for six months.'

'Then we won't make it,' said Mrs Murphy sadly.

'Well, I don't know,' began Mr Murphy while

Max wriggled helplessly. 'If we can catch a plane tonight . . .'

'No, you can't!' shrieked Molly. 'W-what about me and Max?'

'You'll be quite safe here with Professor Slynk,' reassured her dad, while Max struggled to escape from his father's grasp. 'We really need to get the first flight available. We wouldn't stay long – we'd be back practically straight away. But you know how fragile chameleons are. It could be dead before Sylvain gets back.'

Thanks a bunch, thought Max grimly. He tried to twist himself free so that he could hide in the undergrowth.

'Besides,' his dad went on, 'it will be much easier to get two seats than four at such short notice.'

Honestly! thought Max in despair. *When it's something to do with animals, they just can't think of anything else!*

'But you can't leave Max now!' yelled Molly. 'He's – he's not well!'

Just in time, before they asked where he was! *Nice one, Moll!* thought Max.

Immediately, his mum became concerned. 'Oh, poor darling!' she cried. 'I must make sure he's all right. Has he gone to bed? Or,' she narrowed her eyes, 'has he just gone to play on some computer?'

Molly panicked. 'I think it was the heat or something. He's OK really – he just needs a bit of a rest. I'll – I'll look after him.' Actually, it was probably better if nobody tried to find Max. Perhaps she could get him away from her parents while they were booking their plane tickets.

'Well, if you're sure,' said Mrs Murphy doubtfully.

'He'll be fine,' said his father stoutly. 'You know children – up and down like yo-yos. He'll be fit as a fiddle tomorrow. And we haven't any time to waste. If we don't get this chameleon to Sylvain now it could be too late.'

Mrs Murphy didn't look convinced, but her husband grabbed her by the arm and ushered her off, carefully cupping the little chameleon in his other hand.

Molly was almost weeping. 'How can they!' she raged. 'They care more about their horrible animals than about us!'

She followed her parents to the makeshift laboratory and watched in despair as her mum dropped Max into a deep glass tank furnished with little branches and twigs. Mrs Murphy watched the chameleon intently through the glass. Max climbed up a twig and anchored his curled tail round the branch. He tried to disappear, by blending in with the red covers of some books on the shelf behind his tank. He was rather proud that he managed to match the writing on the spine as well! But Mrs Murphy was watching his skin change.

'Sneaky!' she said fondly. 'What a clever little beast you are. But I can still see you.'

'Can I play with it?' asked Molly in despair.

'Don't be silly, dear,' said her mum. 'You know how delicate these creatures are – I'd hate for you to harm it.'

'Yeah, but I was playing with it before and it was OK,' argued Molly desperately.

Mr Murphy was zapping buttons on the telephone at the far end of the lab. 'I'm trying to get through to someone at the airport, but they keep connecting me to the wrong person. Hello? Yes! I'd like to book two seats on a plane to Antananarivo. I need to get there tonight . . .'

If Molly hadn't been so worried about Max she'd have laughed at the anxiety in her dad's voice.

Mrs Murphy fussed about looking for a suitable box to carry the chameleon in. Whenever she turned away, Molly rushed towards the captured Max, but each time her mum swept back before she could get her hand into the tank.

'Molly, if you really want to help you could find me that box of crickets in the cool room. Chameleons love crickets.'

'What, *live* crickets?' gasped Molly.

'Come on, Molly – you know animals usually prefer their food alive,' tutted her mother. 'How often have we told you? That way they can be sure it's completely fresh.'

Yes, but does Max want them completely fresh? thought Molly. She stared into the tank.

Max swivelled his eyes so that he was looking at his mum with one eye and Molly with the other. He winked at her.

'OK, fresh crickets then,' she said crossly. 'Sure you don't want them covered in chocolate?'

Max rapidly turned several shades of purple, uncurled his tail and nearly fell off his branch.

'See? He really hates the idea,' said Molly. But when her mother came to look Max was back on his branch, coloured a nice peaceful green.

'But we simply have to get there tonight!' Mr Murphy was bellowing into the telephone.

'Pass me the tropical reptile spray, please, Molly. And could you make me up a box of wax worms as well?' fussed Mrs Murphy, filling a big nylon-mesh carry cage with branches and green leaves. She leaned over the tank and lifted Max out. 'Come on, little fellow – nobody's going to hurt you. I'm just going to puff a little water on you to keep your skin damp.' She grabbed the spray from Molly and squirted it all over Max.

He'll need clothes when he changes back! thought Molly in panic. She ran to the cold room, looking wildly about her. There were some overalls hanging behind the door. *They'll have to do!* she thought, and tore them down, crumpled them up and stuffed them in a holdall with the boxes of crickets and wax worms.

'That's the best I can do,' she told Max, hoping he would understand.

When she came back, Molly was horrified to see an unwelcome visitor slide into the lab.

'Professor Slynk!' said Mr Murphy, beckoning Slynk towards Max's tank. 'You have to see this.'

Slynk grasped the tank with his hot, pudgy hands and glared down at Max, menacingly.

'Isn't he amazing?' cooed Mrs Murphy. 'Watch – I'll move the tank on to that patterned chair cover and this little chameleon will change to match it.'

'That really would be an amazing transformation,' smirked Slynk. Max willed himself to stay the same colour, though he knew it was hopeless; Slynk was on to him for sure.

'At last!' cried Mr Murphy suddenly. 'Good – good! Thank you!' He put down the telephone and beamed. 'What a fuss when all I wanted was a couple of tickets! Hurry up, Millicent. Our flight leaves in twenty minutes!'

Mr Murphy slipped Max into the small, meshed-sided carry cage, then picked it up. Slynk pretended to help Mrs Murphy with the holdall containing Max's food and the tropical reptile spray.

She didn't see his hand slip inside the bag and release into it a tiny, scuttling robot spy.

4. Flying Lizard

The Murphy's four-wheel drive screeched to a halt by the landing strip. Max bounced about uncomfortably as Mrs Murphy grabbed his cage and the holdall and ran towards the tiny plane.

But, through his cage, Max could see that there was a problem. A man was waving his arms angrily, shouting at an engineer. Max tried to hear what he was saying, but it was in the island language of Malagasy, and he'd only picked up a couple of words since they had arrived. The engineer was spreading his arms out as if to say it was nothing to do with him.

The angry man pointed at the Murphys, jabbing his finger as if he wanted to poke holes in them.

'Oh, dear,' said Mrs Murphy nervously. 'Do you think there's a problem?'

But, now that he had got his precious tickets, Mr Murphy was back to his old absent-minded self. 'Oh, everything will be fine,' he said vaguely.

'Nothing to do with us. Shall we get on?'

Max was shaken again as his mother climbed the steps. She sat down by the window and tucked the cage in by her feet, giving Max another squirt with the reptile spray. Refreshing droplets fell down from the leaves and dripped on to his back. *That's one thing about Mum*, he thought, *she really knows how to look after animals!*

Mr Murphy flopped down beside his wife. He gazed at Max, shaking his head in wonder as the little chameleon obligingly changed colour to match the blue pattern on the carpet. 'What an amazing creature. I bet Sylvain has never seen one like it!'

There were only a few seats in the little aircraft, and one man was already sitting by the window on the other side of the aisle. At the back were several wooden packing cases, each about the height of a door and as wide as a couple of supermarket trolleys. Max could see the gleam of something white and polished between the slats.

'Looks like we're not the only ones bringing cargo,' laughed Mr Murphy, craning his head round to look at the crates. 'I wonder what they are.'

The little aircraft shook slightly as another passenger climbed aboard. It was the angry man they'd seen on the tarmac. He sat down crossly next to the other passenger and they ignored each other grumpily. Max felt sure he'd seen the two of them somewhere before, but he couldn't think where.

'They don't look very happy, do they?' whispered Mrs Murphy. 'I wonder what's wrong.'

They soon found out.

'There's been a bit of a problem,' explained the captain, giving the Murphys a welcoming smile. 'These gentlemen are taking a collection of statues to the Comoros Islands, and they're not too happy that we're going to Antananarivo first. But I've explained there's plenty of time – we'll get to the

Comoros Islands before dark.'

He walked to the front of the plane and began to get ready for the trip. Max could feel the rumbling through his feet as they took off. He wished his parents would lift his cage up a bit higher. All he could see was his mother's sandals.

Mr Murphy leaned over to the other men. 'We're zoology professors,' he explained, 'and we've found an extremely rare chameleon on your island. We have to get to Antananarivo as quickly as possible to see an expert.'

Mrs Murphy leaned over past her husband. 'He's a very famous chameleon expert,' she added. 'We need to see him tonight as he is going away tomorrow morning.'

'So you see, it really is urgent,' said her husband, smiling. He waved his hand at the cage. 'Here he is – nice little creature.'

Max decided it would be a good idea to stay his

normal leafy green colour. Perhaps Malagasies didn't like their chameleons being moved about their island. He didn't want to seem *too* unusual.

Mr Murphy began to tell the men about Max's colour changes and how rare the chameleon was, but the angry man interrupted.

'Let's see!' he growled.

'Come on, little fellow, show the man what you can do,' cooed his parents. Neither of them would dream of poking him, but they did almost everything else. They waved at him, wiggled his leaves about, and jiggled the cage until Max wanted to bite them.

He could easily have changed colour to please them, but he had a gut feeling about these men. They didn't *smell* right.

Suddenly, the angry man got up and poked the cage, jabbing Max with one of his fingers.

'Oh, no, no!' screeched Mrs Murphy. 'You must

never be rough with these little creatures.'

Max couldn't help himself. His skin darkened and he turned a thunderous black with anger. But he didn't turn plain black. He skin was patterned with silver squares that perfectly matched the mesh of his cage.

The angry man seemed amazed. He muttered something to his friend, but Max could only understand the words 'big boss'.

Suddenly, the angry man turned to Mr Murphy, 'How much to buy?' he said.

'Oh, no, he's not for sale,' laughed Mr Murphy. 'We want to study him.'

Max was beginning to wonder which would be worse: to be prodded about in a laboratory by his parents, or sold as a pet to this grumpy passenger.

The angry man glanced out of the window, then jumped up suddenly and began yelling at the pilot.

'Sorry, mate. Only speak English,' said the pilot.

'We have to go to Comoros!' shouted the man. 'We go there first!'

'No can do,' said the pilot pleasantly. 'On the way to the capital now. Got clearance and everything. Don't worry – we'll get you to Comoros in good time.'

'But this is important!' the man protested.

His companion seemed troubled. He kept looking over his shoulder at the crates behind him.

Mrs Murphy looked back, too. What was in there that they were so worried about?

'Are you going to miss a sale or something?' she asked the companion, smiling. 'I do hope not.'

'No,' he growled. Then he seemed to think about it. 'Yes. Miss sale.'

The angry man turned and hissed at his partner, who clamped his mouth shut. In English, he growled, 'It is not possible to go to Antananarivo now. We go to Comoros first, then you come back to Antananarivo.'

'Sorry, mate, but I'm not going all the way to Comoros and coming back again,' said the pilot. 'I've got a date in Comoros tonight.'

Max began to stomp around in his cage. He didn't really care which way round they did it, but really he'd rather not be in an aeroplane when he transformed back to a boy. He could see that if the statue men got their way he might be in trouble.

And there'd be no Molly to help him out of this one!

'Look, he's getting stressed,' said his mother, worried. She got out the tropical reptile spray and squirted Max again.

The angry man was standing beside the pilot wagging a furious finger at him. 'You do as I say!' he bawled.

His friend looked shocked. He jumped up and grabbed hold of the angry man's jacket, trying to pull him back to his seat, but the first man shook him off.

'You see what happen when you not do what I say!' shouted the angry man. His hand went inside his jacket.

'*No* Sata, wait!' his friend cried out in alarm.

But it was too late; Sata had already pulled out a gun.

5. Hijack!

'Oh, but . . .' stuttered Mr Murphy. 'You can't do that!'

'Manfred!' whispered Max's mother. 'Is he going to shoot us all?'

'Silence!' snapped Sata.

Max scurried backwards and forwards along his branch, his tail curling and uncurling so fast that he nearly fell off. Why had he turned into something so small? Why couldn't he have transformed into a lion, or something with really sharp horns? Or even something smaller that was deadly dangerous?

Perhaps he could. Maybe now was the time he'd find out how he did it.

He took a deep breath, shut his strange, conical eyes, and tried to imagine himself into a scorpion. Only he wasn't quite sure what scorpions looked like. He vaguely remembered that they were a bit like tiny lobsters, with a sting in their arched tails. He tried to feel his legs growing a tough, shell-like casing, and another pair of legs growing out of his stomach. Perhaps he could unwind the chameleon tail and turn it the other way?

His stomach began to ache, and his tail twitched. He almost, *almost*, felt as if it had worked. But when he opened his eyes again he could only see his little chameleon feet clutching at the branch his mum had put there for him to perch on, and his long chameleon tail coiled round it. He was so cross that his skin turned black all over.

'Look, Manfred,' he could hear his mother cooing. 'He's getting angry again.'

Mum, your plane's being hijacked, and all you can think of is how I'm changing colour! Max thought in despair. He tried to puff himself up so that he looked big and threatening. Maybe those thugs would think he was a poisonous lizard and keep away. He pushed at the mesh of his cage, trying to make them think he could burst through.

'Look at it now!' he could hear his father saying. 'I've never seen a chameleon do that either. Sylvain will be *so* interested!'

If we ever get there! thought Max in panic. He didn't like the look of the men at all. Sata was still standing beside the pilot and threatening him with the gun.

'Don't be stupid,' the pilot was saying calmly. 'If you shoot me who's going to land the plane?'

Obviously, the men hadn't thought of that.

'Plus,' the pilot went on, 'if you shoot any of us

you'll probably make a nasty hole in the plane as well, then all the air suddenly rushing in will depressurise the aircraft. Had you thought of that? Sure way to make us crash.'

Max went cold at the thought of the plane diving out of the sky, turning them all into a rather nasty mess on the ground beneath.

'And now he's gone blue,' said Mrs Murphy, looking at Max admiringly. 'Don't they realise how important it is for us to get him to Sylvain tonight?'

What's so important about the statues? Max wondered. *Why do they have to be delivered so quickly? They must be very valuable for the men to risk holding up the pilot and the other passengers.*

Sata's friend stood up. He was jabbering away in Malagasy, waving his hands about. Sata looked at the Murphys and nodded. 'OK, Manaitra.'

Oh, no, what now? thought Max.

He found out very soon.

'This way,' said Manaitra, yanking at Mr Murphy's arm and pulling him towards the back of the plane.

'But . . .' stuttered his father.

Do as they say, Dad! Max wanted to scream, but nothing came out of his wide chameleon mouth except his long tongue.

'Oh, look – he's hungry,' said Mrs Murphy anxiously. 'Excuse me – I don't know why you want us to go back there, but let me feed him first.' She began to pull down the holdall with the crickets and wax worms from the luggage rack.

'Not wait. Not feed. You go now!'

'Yes, yes, of course,' said Mrs Murphy. She grabbed the handle of the cage with trembling hands.

'Leave lizard,' commanded Manaitra.

'Certainly not. I'm not leaving this animal. Don't you understand, it's *rare!*' said Mrs Murphy in a shaky voice. 'There's never been a chameleon like this before!'

'Not lizard,' insisted Manaitra, trying to push her towards Mr Murphy.

'You should care about it – it comes from your island!' she scolded.

'You go to back!' shouted Manaitra.

'Not without my chameleon!' shouted Mrs Murphy in return. She stood up clutching Max's cage to her chest.

Nice to be wanted, thought Max bitterly, *even if they don't know they're really protecting their son!* He swung about in the half darkness as his mother cradled the cage in her arms.

Manaitra glared at Mrs Murphy. He reached into his pocket. Through the gap in his mother's arms Max could see the glint of a knife blade.

'Millicent! Do as he says!' pleaded her husband. 'The animal will be all right.'

No, I won't! Max wanted to shout. He could see the hijacker moving towards him and that shining knife blade getting closer and closer. He could hear it scraping on the mesh of his cage.

'*Nooo!*' screamed Mrs Murphy.

'Then you do what you are told.' Manaitra held out his hand for the cage. 'You go to back. I look after lizard.'

'A-all right,' stammered Mrs Murphy. 'But you mustn't hurt it, you hear me?'

Manaitra snatched the cage from her and grinned at Sata who left the pilot and joined Manaitra at the back of the plane. 'Will please big boss,' he said in English. Max started to wonder who this 'big boss' might be, but he was interrupted with a thump, as Manaitra dumped his cage down heavily on to a seat. Unfortunately, the branch wasn't very firmly fixed to the cage, and Max fell to the bottom with his tail still firmly wound round it.

But from there he could just see through the gap in the seats.

They couldn't be – surely not!

The two men were tying up his parents, back to back, as they sat on the floor of the plane. Their hands and feet were trussed like parcels.

'Now you stay quiet,' hissed Sata, waving his gun menacingly at them.

Max rattled his cage furiously, but Manaitra sneered at him as he marched back towards the front of the plane. Max swivelled one of his eyes and watched. He was going up to the pilot! He spoke in Malagasy, but it was quite clear what he wanted. The pilot shook his head, but it was no good. Manaitra had grabbed hold of the control stick.

'Don't you dare do that!' yelled the pilot. 'You can't fly this plane!'

There was a jeering laugh from the back. With his other eye still glued to the gap in the seats, Max

saw Sata wave his gun in triumph.

The pilot swore, and tried to wrestle the stick away from Manaitra. The plane lurched, and Mrs Murphy screamed as it swerved violently to the left.

The cage slid across the seats and fell against the side of the plane. Max gasped as he tumbled upside down. He heard Sata give a shout, and then the cage was sent flying again as Manaitra raced to the back of the plane.

Max's side hurt where he had landed and he began to feel very sick. Then he heard his father shout, 'Millicent – roll over.'

The falling crate missed his mother by centimetres. The thin wood splintered as the statue inside crashed on to the floor of the plane. Max could hear it even over the roar of the engine.

The head of the statue rolled down the aisle towards him. Out of it tumbled streams of tiny red and green gems.

6. Rubies and Emeralds

Max stared in wonder as the streams trickled closer to him, then stopped.

Why were the statues filled with glass beads? Did it make them stand up better or something?

And then he remembered Molly telling him about the shipment of precious jewels that had disappeared somewhere between Kuala Lumpur and Zambia.

Rubies and emeralds. That was what they were. Red and green gems that, if you didn't know better, might look like coloured glass beads.

Wow! Max thought to himself. *I'm looking at a fortune!*

So were the hijackers. Max would have laughed at their faces if he'd been able to laugh. Their expressions showed a mixture of horror and panic.

Suddenly, Sata flung himself to the floor and began scooping up the jewels in great handfuls. For a moment, he sat back on his heels, helplessly wondering what to do with them. Then he shoved them in his pocket, and started trying to dig out the gems that had fallen between the floor and the carpet that ran down between the seats.

Of course, thought Max. *That's why they were so upset when Mum and Dad said they had to go to Antananarivo first. These jewels are stolen! They've got to get them to the Comoros Islands quickly. I bet every plane that goes into the airport will be searched. And they know it! They don't want to go anywhere near Antananarivo.*

Manaitra panicked. He kept trying to wrench the controls from the pilot.

'Get out of my cockpit!' roared the pilot, smacking the hijacker across the face.

The hijacker punched the pilot in return, and the plane rocked dangerously.

Max missed the rest of the fight, as his cage went tumbling off the seat into the aisle. The metal frame was already bent, and the crash on to the floor made it buckle still more. Some of the mesh tore away from the frame and the twigs and leaves of Max's branch poked out of the hole.

The plane swung from side to side, until Sata roared at his friend to stop. There was a stream of bad-tempered Malagasy, then Manaitra sulkily joined Sata trying to pick up the rest of the jewels.

They weren't looking at Max. He could see them scrabbling on the floor, intent on getting up as many of the gems as possible. They weren't taking any

notice of their captives either. Sata wasn't waving a gun at them any more. Max could see his parents struggling to free themselves. Perhaps he could do something to help them? At least he could get out of the cage now. He'd think what to do then.

Carefully, slowly, he crawled out of the damaged cage. It wasn't so easy. The broken bit was at the top, so he needed to climb up on the branch first, then try to push his little body through the gap which was full of leaves and twigs.

Manaitra looked round. Max froze. Sata growled something and Manaitra replied, then picked up the gun and stomped back to the cockpit.

'You do what my friend say,' Sata shouted over to the pilot.

'OK, mate, OK,' answered the pilot wearily.

Max wondered if the pilot was really going to obey and take the smugglers to the Comoros Islands. He couldn't see out of the window, but the plane was very small. It wouldn't be flying very high. The hijackers would be able to see where the pilot was going.

The two men turned back to what they were doing. Manaitra occasionally waved his gun towards Max's parents, but most of the time he was busily picking up the gemstones.

Cautiously, Max managed to wriggle his way out of the cage. He felt quite weak. He needed food. *I wish Sata had let Mum feed me before he tied her up*, he thought.

With clawed feet he could grip the seat coverings quite well. He swivelled one of his eyes towards his back and was very pleased that his new colour was an exact match.

He could see his mother's eye on him. He winked at her, as he had at Molly earlier, to show her he was here and trying to do something to help. But, of course, Mum didn't catch on. She just smiled in wonder, thinking this was another lovely thing about the strangely different chameleon.

Bit by bit, he slowly drew nearer. Suddenly, the hijacker shouted and Max went rigid. But Sata was only talking to Manaitra in the cockpit.

'What a clever little beast!' he heard his father say quietly, and he realised that Dad's eyes were right on him. Swiftly, Max did several colour changes before going back to the dark grey-blue of the plane's seat covers.

'It's being a bit too brave,' whispered his mother. 'I'd have been happier if it had stayed in its cage.'

'Don't be silly, Millicent,' said Mr Murphy. 'It's only natural for a wild animal to escape if it can. But I'm really amazed at the way it's coming over to us – it's almost as if it's trying to comfort us!'

Max stared at his father, who was still wriggling to free himself. *Come on, Dad,* he wanted to say. *Tell me what to do!*

62

'I do believe it's trying to rescue us,' breathed Mrs Murphy. 'How foolish! As if a little thing like that could help us!'

Yeah, Mum, but I haven't done anything yet, thought Max desperately.

Suddenly, he saw Sata's cruel eye on him and, in panic, he turned back to leaf green.

Sata shouted something to Manaitra in the cockpit, and his friend shouted back.

'Oh, no, please . . .' cried Max's mother.

Max turned – too late.

He could feel a tug at his tail, then worse – far worse. His tail felt as if it were coming out at the roots, and he was whooshed up into the air as if someone was hauling him up a cliff.

Dangling in front of the hijacker's shirt buttons. Max could smell the stink of the man's sweat. His feet scrabbled uselessly in the air, but the man only held his tail tighter.

All Max could hear were his mother's screams, but he could *see* the thing she was screaming at all right.

It was the knife, its blade shining in the interior lights.

He's going to cut me in two, thought Max and his skin turned deep yellow. But Sata wasn't looking at the little chameleon at all. He was staring intently at Max's parents.

'One more word, I kill you. Understand?'

The knife glinted horribly, as Sata moved it closer to Mrs Murphy's throat.

7. A Sticky Situation

Max felt as if his tail was being torn off. He wanted to scream, but no sound came out of his mouth. He whipped his little body from side to side, trying to escape. His hands and feet scrabbled uselessly at the air. He couldn't even reach the man's hand to give it a scratch! He just needed something to distract Sata's attention from his parents.

'*Stop! Stop!*'

It was Manaitra. 'Big boss not want trouble. Just want jewels and lizard.'

There was a burst of Malagasy speech between Manaitra and Sata. Then Sata stopped swinging Max around and let the knife drop.

Max's chameleon head whirred. He sensed, rather than saw, his parents holding their breath as the hijackers shouted to each other across the plane. Then there was a lot of nodding, and Sata gripped the knife and pointed it threateningly at Max.

'You *can't*!' whispered Mrs Murphy.

'*No,*' Manaitra shouted from the cockpit. 'Big boss want lizard alive.'

'OK, little lizard. You live.' Wearily, Sata put him down on to the floor of the plane. Max was too busy thinking to worry about changing his skin to the colour of the carpet, but all by itself he could feel a colour change. *Who is this big boss?* he wondered. *What does he want with a chameleon, and how does he know I'm on the plane?* He moved one eye to look at his back. He had turned yellow with the stripes on his back a deeper greenish-yellow, as if a child had coloured him in with crayons.

Max moved off to the side of the plane. He had seen a tarpaulin over there. A good place to hide. He wished he could have moved a bit faster but his chameleon legs would only go at chameleon speed. It seemed to take *years*. And he was still starving! Maybe he was so slow because he needed food.

A fly buzzed past his face and, without thinking about it, his sticky tongue shot out and sucked it back into his mouth. He blinked. *Yuck!* He was actually *eating* a fly!

His jaws crunched down and the fly juices flowed into his throat. Actually, it tasted OK! Like a kind of chameleon crisp.

And it was obviously brain food too as, suddenly, Max knew exactly what he had to do next.

Sata put down his knife. His hostages were quiet, and the lizard had crawled off. He wasn't sure what to do first: chase after the lizard, or get the jewels back into the statue. Well, at least he knew the chameleon couldn't escape from the plane.

The hijacker scrabbled around on the floor, pushing out more tiny gems from where the seats were bolted to the floor. He picked up the broken statue and began to drop the gems from his pockets into its hollow legs.

Quietly, slowly, Max crawled back. He was careful to match his skin colour to every change of colour on the floor. He felt especially proud of the way he walked over the metal strip down the centre of the plane. He could feel the colour changes flow down his skin.

Then he saw the knife.

He stopped, completely still. He was just a slight bulge on the carpet. Sata was completely absorbed in his packing.

Like lightning, Max's tongue shot out and moved it. The knife was small, but heavier than he'd expected. Max froze. But Sata hadn't noticed anything.

His tongue was back in his mouth, ready to spring again. This time Max knew how heavy the knife was going to be. Pity he hadn't had a bit of practice with crickets first. But his chameleon brain knew how to get it this time.

The tongue flicked. The sticky pad on the end caught the knife and whipped it back towards him carefully – he didn't want to pull the blade inside his mouth!

He uncoiled his tail and managed to wrap it round the knife. Then he crawled back along the carpet to the side of the plane. He could see where he could climb up – the ribs of the walls were a perfect 'tree' for his little clawed feet. And the luggage racks would be a really good place to hide. Once they realised he had their knife, there was every chance the hijackers would change their minds about keeping him alive.

He watched the people down below with one eye as he slowly made his way upwards. His parents had their mouths open in wonder. He swaggered a bit as he reached the luggage rack and nearly fell off. Making sure he was holding on properly with his feet, and that they were still watching him, he

waved the knife with his tail. It was as much as his parents could do not to laugh, it looked so comical.

With a grunt, Sata sat back on his heels. He felt for his knife.

It wasn't there.

He looked round, more and more frantically. He scrabbled about the floor, sweeping his hand across the carpet. Manaitra called over to him, and he rasped something in reply, looking over to the Murphys.

'You take?' he growled. But Max's parents obviously didn't have it. They were still tightly tied up, back to back.

Unfortunately, they were still watching Max.

Sata followed their gaze.

Max whipped the knife down into the luggage rack, but it was too late.

Sata yelled. He leaned over the seats, reaching for the rack – and Max. He grabbed at the knife, but the blade was pointing towards him. He swore and flapped at the chameleon, trying to grab it.

The hijacker's flailing arm whacked at Max. His feet lost their grip, and he felt his balance go. Scrabbling frantically, he felt himself begin to tumble out of the luggage rack.

But Max wasn't the only thing that was tumbling. Sata had knocked into Mrs Murphy's open holdall in the luggage rack, and a tiny, metal insect had fallen out. It hit the floor and scuttled under the seat. No one but Max had noticed.

Suddenly, the penny dropped, and Max remembered where he'd seen Sata and Manaitra before. It was in the lobby of the hotel back in Madagascar. They had been talking to . . .

I'm such an idiot, thought Max as he looked desperately for something to break his fall. *I should have known all along that only one person could possibly be behind all this: Professor Preston Slynk.*

8. Hoppy Landings

'N*oooo!*' Max could hear his mother's scream as he flailed desperately, trying to hook his feet into the edge of the luggage rack. Luckily, his fall was a short one. He managed to grab the holdall strap with his front feet, and swung for a while, tormenting his captors by waving the knife at them. Brilliant light from outside the plane flashed off the blade and sent little reflecting darts on to the walls inside.

This is cool! he thought. *Mum would be proud of me — if only she knew who I was!*

Then disaster struck. Max wasn't properly anchored. The weight of the knife unbalanced him and the strap slid out of his grappling claws. His tail uncurled, ready to coil again round the strap and the knife dropped, thunking down between the seat and the side of the plane. His tail missed the strap and he grabbed frantically with his front feet, but the plane lurched and he was falling again.

Max felt himself drop, over and over. Then, with a thump, he hit the top of a seat. His claws grabbed at the fabric, and he hung on grimly. But still he hadn't properly got his balance back. Slowly, he toppled down the back of the seat, trying to hook a claw in *anywhere*, but feeling the seat cover tear out of his grasp as he fell.

His breath was knocked right out of him as he landed on the carpet. He stayed still as a rock for

several minutes, waiting for Sata's hairy hands to grab him.

But after seeing his knife fall harmlessly out of the way, the hijacker had gone back to scooping up the jewels and thrusting them into the broken statue. He seemed in a panic to get it done quickly. Were they coming in to Antananarivo? Or – Max's little heart jumped – had they got to the Comoros Islands?

Max looked over at his parents. They were whispering to each other, their ears brushing together as they tried to turn their heads to get eye contact. Both of them were looking over in his direction, with big grins on their faces.

Oh, come on, Mum and Dad! Max thought in despair. *Stop looking at me!*

As if they could hear him, they turned their faces away from each other again.

OK, now stay like that! he wanted to tell them. And hoping that they would understand what he was going to try and do, he crawled along the aisle of the plane, carefully changing colour to match every surface.

In the cockpit, Manaitra was still holding the gun against the pilot's head. Moving as fast as he could,

Max eased himself on to the co-pilot's seat, taking the pattern on to his skin.

Now that he was here, he didn't have the faintest clue what to do. He wished Molly was with him. She was always full of ideas.

For the first time now, he could see out. They certainly weren't coming in to Antananarivo. Down below there was water, lots of it. And a small island covered with a fuzz of trees. He could hear the engine note change, and a grunt of satisfaction from Manaitra. The pilot must be coming down to land on one of the Comoros Islands.

Max had to stop the men from getting away with their smugglers' hoard! But more than that, he had to save his parents. They were alive, but who knew what would happen after the plane landed! The only reason they hadn't been shot so far was because the hijackers didn't want the plane to crash.

The plane was losing height rapidly. Through the

cockpit window, Max could see houses; he could see cars driving along tiny, snaking roads. He had to stop the hijackers landing where their friends were waiting for them. And he had to do it quickly. He gulped and his little legs tensed. Ready, and . . .

He jumped, right up on to Manaitra's head!

The man screeched. His arms seesawed frantically, trying to shove Max off his face. The gun waved dangerously.

'Well done, little chap,' grinned the pilot, amazed.

Max took aim and waited for the right moment. Manaitra was still trying to wipe the chameleon from his face when suddenly his fingers loosened on the gun and Max flicked out his sticky tongue and lashed his tail. The gun fell from Manaitra's hand and slid over to the other side of the cockpit.

The hijacker snarled as he felt the gun whip away from his hand. He used both hands to claw at Max, trying to pull the little animal away. But Max

80

hung on, digging his claws into the soft skin of the man's cheeks, feeling furiously glad at the hijacker's screams. He could see people on the ground now, and the roofs were getting dangerously close. Then he spotted two things: a tiny landing strip, and a battered jeep half hidden in the bushes. As he watched, two men got out of the jeep, ran to the edge of the landing strip and waved upwards.

Without thinking, Max jumped from Manaitra's face to the pilot's knee and grasped the control stick with his tail, wrenching it to the left. The plane lurched and almost turned on to its wing tip. The hijacker moaned with fear, and Sata screamed from the back.

'What the –?' screeched the pilot. 'Get off! You'll kill us all!' Max could feel his hand trembling as, sweeping Max aside, he grasped the controls again. Shaking, he managed to straighten the plane. 'Right, everyone,' he said grimly, and Max could hear the tremble in his voice as he tried to steady both himself and the plane, 'seat belts on, NOW. I'm going to have to land in a field. Sit down and prepare for crash landing. Arms over your heads!'

He didn't wait to see if they had obeyed his orders. He was too busy fighting to get the plane down in one piece. Outside, Max could see men running around. Then the landing strip disappeared under the plane, and they were hurtling towards the trees. He could see the field rushing towards them. Were they going too fast to land in it? He could hear the pilot swearing under his breath as he fought with his controls.

Too late, Max realised what he might have done. His parents were tied back to back. No way could they protect their heads with their arms. They weren't buckled to their seats; they were unprotected, on the floor.

If the plane crashed, it would be all his fault.

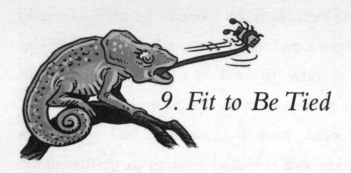

9. Fit to Be Tied

With a great noise and shudder, the plane was down. Max was bounced up and down on the co-pilot's seat as the craft seemed to hop up and down again and again. There was a ghastly screaming noise as it skidded along the ground, jerking as the nose hit rocks. Then, all at once, there came a horrible crunching sound from beneath the plane.

'Wheel's gone!' said the pilot through gritted teeth.

Sata and Manaitra slid forwards, screaming. Max couldn't hear his parents, and even with his moveable eyes he couldn't see them at the back of the plane.

Then, through the cockpit window, he saw a huge pile of earth begin to gather in front of them, until the weight of it was so great it slowed the little plane to a stop.

'Never, never, let this happen to me again ...' the dazed pilot was muttering.

Groggily, Max crawled up the co-pilot seat and looked over the back of it. Behind him, Manaitra mopped a cut on his head. Sata was swearing furiously, waving his hands towards the back of the plane. The statues had all fallen. Gleaming white arms, legs and bodies were mixed up with splinters of crate. And a cascade of sapphires, diamonds and emeralds was spilling out all over the floor.

Mum and Dad! Max thought, scanning the plane

wildly for some sign of them.

They seemed to have disappeared. But how could they? Max's heart beat unpleasantly fast as his eyes swivelled, searching this way and that.

He crawled down from the seat, forgetting to change colours as he went. Once he was on the floor, he could see his parents at last. When the plane had nose-dived they had slid forwards. They were both jammed behind the back seats. The tumbling statues had missed them by centimetres. Mrs Murphy was sobbing quietly and Mr Murphy was mumbling under his breath. They were in a state of total shock, but they were alive!

Then Max heard the pilot yelling. Manaitra was busily tying him to the seat. Sata was scooping up as many of the jewels as he could and stuffing them frantically into the broken bases of the statues. Manaitra soon joined him, ignoring the pilot's frantic shouts.

'You won't get away with this!' he was yelling. 'Everyone will have seen us come down – they'll be here to rescue us!'

Yeah, but don't tell them that, thought Max as he scurried across the floor to make sure his parents were not hurt.

The hijackers obviously knew they were in trouble, though. They shouted at each other in Malagasy, rushing to rescue their jewels, and looking out of the aircraft windows in panic.

Then, just as Max had checked his parents and seen that they were only bruised, he heard a triumphant yell from behind him. No! He'd forgotten to change colour! He felt the familiar sickness as he was lifted up in Sata's big hand.

'Now I tell big boss I have jewels *and* lizard,' he said, leering at Max's parents. With an evil grin he grabbed Mrs Murphy's holdall with the crickets and wax worms (and the overalls that Molly had thrown in with them at the last minute), shaking it in her face. 'You not need worry. I feed him. Keep him alive for big boss.'

Manaitra growled something in Malagasy. Max instinctively knew it wasn't friendly. He sniggered inside, remembering how he'd clawed at Manaitra's face. And then, suddenly, he couldn't see anything at all as Sata covered him with a smelly blanket.

Hot, suffocating and uncomfortable, Max felt the sickening bump as Sata jumped out of the broken plane. His stomach churned as the men ran over the uneven ground. He heard car doors slam, gasped as Sata threw him into a corner under his blanket, then he heard an engine whirr and spark into life.

As the vehicle roared away, Max managed to poke his head out from underneath the blanket. He was in a jeep, bouncing over a dirt road through dense forest. And faintly, very faintly, he could hear police sirens.

If they go off this road the police will never find us, he thought. *Got to slow them down!*

Carefully, he crawled up the back of the driver's seat then, suddenly, Max leapt on the man's head, grabbing at his face with his sharp claws.

The driver shrieked and the jeep zigzagged all over the road. Sata and Manaitra yelled at him, and the fourth man tried to grab the wheel as Manaitra lunged over the seat in an attempt to catch the chameleon. But Max jumped off the driver's face and crept down to hide himself under the seat, turning his skin a dingy brown colour to match the dirt on the floor. *If I can just get under the pedal* . . . he thought, desperately. *So long as I don't get squashed*, he added grimly to himself. He crawled forwards to try and wedge himself under the accelerator pedal.

Sata yelled at the other three as the driver swore and swung the wheel dangerously. There was a splintering *crrrunch*. Max was thrown back under the seat. It felt as though they'd hit a tree or something. As they moved off again, there came a metallic clatter. It sounded as if something had dropped off the jeep!

Manaitra growled fiercely. It wasn't long before Max realised what he was saying. He bent down to the floor of the jeep and started grabbing wildly, searching for the little chameleon. Max stayed frozen, hoping his colours would save him again. But they wouldn't help him if the man touched the warm texture of his body. The smuggler groped again, his voice clearly cursing and swearing.

The sirens were getting nearer. If Max could slow them down just that bit more . . .

'*Ah!*' There was a roar of triumph. Max felt a hand grab his tail uncomfortably tightly, then lift him up. Sata shook his head and clucked like an old hen, saying something that sounded pretty disapproving in Malagasy.

He was back under his blanket and Sata's big, hairy hand was making quite sure he couldn't crawl out this time.

It wasn't long before the jeep stopped, the men got out, and Max suffered another bumpy run under the suffocating blanket.

Sata yanked off the blanket and held Max up by his tail. He was showing Max off and telling the others about him in Malagasy. He seemed to be blaming Max for everything. The men laughed unpleasantly and Max shivered. What were they going to do with him?

They were dumping the legs and feet of several statues down in a corner. Manaitra grunted something and the others nodded. *They're arranging for the stuff to be collected*, thought Max. But he was wrong. Manaitra pulled some string out of his pocket and tied one end of it round Max's neck, fastening it in a neat bow. He looked around, and one of the other men laughed and pointed to a hefty looking wooden table that was just centimetres away from Max.

Manaitra grinned. *Oh, no!* Max struggled, but he couldn't escape from his captor.

Sata dumped the holdall containing the crickets,

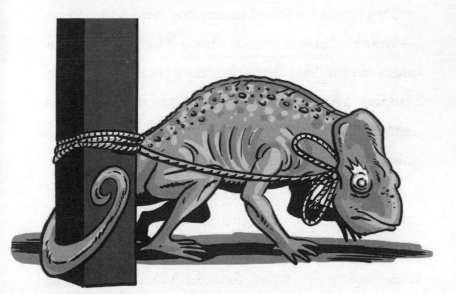

wax worms and reptile spray beside Max. He pulled out the box of crickets, and the overalls that Molly had shoved in with them came out with it.

Max shot out his tongue. After all he *was* a chameleon, and he was starving! The cricket that Sata fed him crunched. It was like biting into a stick of celery.

Meanwhile, back at the hotel in Madagascar, Molly was waiting nervously by the phone in her room, hoping for news from Max. And in his room just down the corridor, Preston Slynk looked at his watch then jabbed a number into his mobile.

He sat back and waited for an answer.

Sata's mobile rang suddenly and all eyes in the room – including Max's – turned to watch him.

'Yes, boss?' he said.

'Well?' demanded a man at the other end of the line. The sound echoed around the empty warehouse and Max recognised the voice from just one word. But he already knew that 'big boss' was really Professor Stink.

'We get jewels and lizard,' answered Sata, before the phone went dead.

Even though he'd joked with Molly about the idea of Slynk stealing the jewels, he knew better than to be surprised by the professor's involvement in the theft. He'd learnt from experience that Slynk was capable of just about anything – and he had an annoying knack of getting away with things.

If only the police could catch Stink red-handed, Max thought. He strained his ears hoping to hear the police sirens again, but all was quiet.

Suddenly, Max felt his skin stretch. There was a most peculiar feeling in his rear end. *Must be because they kept picking me up by the tail*, he thought. He turned one of his eyes to look, as the other eye watched the next cricket struggling out of the cool box.

His back was changing. The chameleon colours were turning to a slightly tanned pink. And his tail felt like it was being sucked into his behind. *Oh, no, I'm going to get strangled!* thought Max in panic, as the string tightened round his neck. Why did he have to change back now? Max wished he had more control over his transformations. He clawed at the string with his front feet and managed to pull the end that would undo the bow. He felt his little feet lengthen, the claws flattening and changing to his familiar rather dirty and bitten fingernails. His backwards-facing eye swivelled.

'*Ouch!*' said Max, as it yanked itself back to

match the other front-facing eye. He rubbed his neck. The cricket taste was still in his throat. It wasn't all that bad! But it was good to feel there was room in his mouth now that his tongue had shrunk back to its proper size.

He put his hands out for the overalls. They were *huge*. Crossly, he wrapped them round himself. Why couldn't Molly have found something to fit him?

His body filled out, and his chameleon feet lengthened. *Oh, well, it could be worse*, Max thought, as he rolled up the legs and sleeves to fit.

Then Sata turned and saw him.

10. Victory!

M ax knew what the hijacker must be saying. His expression said it all: 'I don't believe it!'

He gave the men a little wave.

Sata shrieked something in Malagasy. Max couldn't believe it either!

He shrugged, which seemed to infuriate Sata.

The man who had tied him to the table had his mouth open in shocked surprise. He kept gulping and pointing. The driver shouted at him, and walked angrily over to Max. He tipped out the bag of crickets, which hopped gleefully around the floor of the warehouse. He made a stabbing gesture at them. The lizard has escaped, he seemed to say, run away like these crickets.

His friend was still gobsmacked, shaking his head from side to side.

Sata was shrieking into Max's face, but it was in Malagasy and he hadn't a clue what the man was saying. He only knew that his breath stank. Then Sata changed his language. 'You, lizard boy,' he demanded. 'Big boss tell me all about you. I not believe him – till now.'

Before Max could think of a clever reply, there was a loud splintering noise. All heads whipped round towards the door, which was slowly falling apart before their gaze.

Max heaved a sigh of relief. He *had* managed to slow down the smugglers enough for the police

to follow them. But they were only just in time.

The policemen's orders rattled out like machine-gun fire. One of the smugglers dropped his gun. It clattered on to the concrete. Slowly, the other smugglers raised their hands above their heads. A policeman glared at Max and snapped another command at him.

Half a dozen other officers followed and stood grimly with their guns trained on the smugglers. Their eyes popped slightly seeing Max in his enormous overalls.

Max raised his hands. 'I'm not . . .' he began, but Manaitra did it for him.

'He no with us. He come here self,' insisted Manaitra, but the man who had tied up Max obviously understood English too.

'He lizard. He chameleon!'

'You smuggle boy!' snarled Manaitra to Sata, then repeated himself in Malagasy to make sure his friend had understood.

'*Lizard!*' protested Sata.

'You stop telling lie,' shouted Manaitra. 'You smuggle boy on plane. Now you tell me he lizard! You tell police why you do it.'

They were still bawling accusations at each other when the police snapped handcuffs on them all.

A pair of cuffs shone in front of Max's appalled face. 'No, I'm Max. Max Murphy,' he explained. 'My parents were on the plane – they'll tell you who I am.'

The policeman looked suspicious. 'They said nothing about a boy,' he said, glaring at Max's overalls. 'Only a valuable chameleon.'

'Yeah, well . . .' said Max.

'You'd better come with us,' said the policeman, taking Max firmly by the arm. 'Perhaps your parents will recognise you.' From the way he spoke, Max knew that the policeman didn't think *that* was very likely.

'Er – can we take the crickets with us, sir?' said Max.

'Max! How on earth did you get here?' Mrs Murphy looked her son up and down in the too-large overalls. She seemed shaken from her ordeal and started at the sight of Max.

'Yeah, well, I was with you all the time,' he said truthfully.

'Max!' warned his father.

'Well, I sort of wanted to come with you,' said Max.

'But you were ill!' said his mother. 'Molly told me you'd gone to bed!'

'I came down when you were getting the cage

ready,' Max was thinking quickly. He pulled at the lapel of his overalls to prove he'd been in the lab. 'And I thought . . .'

'You wanted to show Sylvain the chameleon!' said his mother fondly, ruffling his hair. Max wished she wouldn't do that. 'Wasn't it wonderful! I do hope that nice policeman has managed to find it.'

'I don't understand,' said his father. 'Why didn't you tell us you were on the plane?'

Max shrugged. 'I was going to, but things got a bit scary and I thought there was no point in all of us getting tied up. I hid at the back, behind those statues.'

'Statues!' said his mother darkly. 'They were *smuggling jewels!*' She looked shocked at the very idea. 'Thank goodness I didn't know you were there when we crashed!' she added. 'It was very naughty of you, Max!'

'But how did those men get hold of you?' said his father, puzzled. 'I didn't see them take anyone out of that plane wreck!'

'But we were still tied up, remember!' said Mrs Murphy, clutching at Max's arm.

'I was making sure you were all right,' said Max, almost truthfully. 'Then they saw me and grabbed me – as a hostage, I suppose, just in case . . .'

'I still don't . . .' said Mr Murphy.

But his wife said urgently, 'Now that we're sure that Max is all right, I think we should go and look for the chameleon.' She stared over at the warehouse where some policemen were trying to shove the smugglers into their cars. 'Do you think one of them might still have it in a pocket or something?'

'Oh – er – it got away,' said Max. 'I saw it escape. We'll never find it again. I saw it head for the trees.'

'Oh, dear,' said his mother sadly. 'And I so wanted to write down everything about it for our book. And when Sylvain hears about it, he'll be so disappointed. Still, I suppose the forest is really the best place for it. I wonder how it will get on in the Comoros Islands instead of Madagascar.'

'At least everyone is safe now,' said Mr Murphy. He looked at Max and frowned. 'I ought to be very annoyed with you, Max, but I guess you've been badly frightened by all this.'

'Just remember, you must *always* tell us if you're coming with us,' said his mother sternly.

'Yes, Mum.' Max was glad his parents were always so vague. He didn't want to explain what had *really* happened. He shuddered to think what they might do to him to find out *how* it happened!

'And I think we really ought to go back home,' his mother was saying as they waited for one of the policemen to give them a lift back to the airstrip.

'You mean, real home?' said Max. 'Not just the hotel?'

Back to proper things like computer games and school and crisps. But he couldn't wait to get to the hotel first to tell Molly how he had saved their parents from a gang of hijackers!

He also wanted to see the look on her face when he told her that they'd been right about Slynk from the start. He really was mixed up with the jewel thieves. If only Slynk had been in the warehouse when the police had arrived. By now they'd be locking him up and Max would only have his transformations to worry about.

Maybe I should tell the police about him? Max thought. But he knew if he tried to tell anyone about Slynk, they'd soon find out Max's secret and he just couldn't take that risk.

Then another thought struck Max, and he had to laugh. When he was a chameleon and ate the

fly, his brain suddenly became clear as glass. He'd known exactly what to do. Supposing he swallowed a few of the leftover crickets before his next maths test — would it make his brain able to work out those sums he wasn't very good at?

It was worth a try.

More Classic Chameleon Facts!

They may be deaf! It's clear they don't have outer ears but, unlike some other reptiles, chameleons don't seem to have inner ears either.

They sway! Chameleons can move very slow and rhythmically in order to mimic the movement of a leaf or branch.

They have long tongues! In fact, some chameleons' tongues are longer than their bodies! And they have sticky tips, so they can catch their prey effectively.

They've got super-strong jaws! A chameleon's jaws are so strong, even a tiny one is capable of crushing a large insect such as a locust.

They love sunbathing! When exposed to the sun, chameleons behave in a more sociable way and are more likely to mate and reproduce. So you might say that they are solar powered!

They're a big family! Scientists think that about 134 species of chameleons exist.

They're clingy! Chameleons have a prehensile tail, meaning it can be used to grip things.

How Changeable Are You?

Are you as changeable as the British weather? Check out your inner chameleon with this cracking chameleon quiz . . .

1. Do you have a favourite colour?

A It depends on my mood

B Yes – and it's always been the same

C Yes – I've recently changed it

2. On an average Saturday, how many times do you change your clothes?

A It depends on what I'm doing

B Two or three – but usually first thing when I'm trying to decide what to wear

C None – Saturday is pyjamas day

3. Are you moody?

A No, I'm always happy

B Yes, friends and family never know where they are with me

C I'm grumpy most of the time

4. How often do you change your socks?

A Every day

B As infrequently as possible

C Whenever I'm told to

5. How many of the following sayings do you agree with?

A Some things never change

B A change is as good as a rest

C A leopard can't change its spots

Scores

1. A = 2 B = 0 C = 1
2. A = 1 B = 2 C = 0
3. A = 0 B = 2 C = 1

4. A = 2 B = 0 C = 1
5. **SCORE 1 POINT FOR EACH SAYING YOU AGREE WITH**

Conclusions

If you scored 0–3 points, you're a **Calmer Chameleon** — cool, collected and not prone to moodiness or changeability. All well and good on the mood front — but those socks are going to be walking to the laundry basket on their own if you don't do something about them!

If you scored 4–7 points, you're a **Kind Chameleon**. You're likeable, fun and unpredictable. Your spontaneous nature makes you very popular, but your sudden bad moods can sometimes confuse the people around you. Try to smile more!

If you scored 8–11 points, you're **King Chameleon** — the most changeable of them all! Your moods are up and down like a yo-yo, you change your mind every five minutes and your hairstyle every week. You're a laugh to be around — even if not many people can keep up with you!

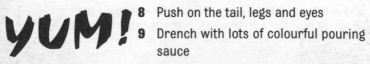

UNCLE HERBERT'S COOL CHAMELEON

Uncle Herbert did try a version of this using sticky rice instead of ice cream, but we think this one is far more delicious. Quick! Scoff it down before it melts!

YOU'LL NEED:

A packet of coloured fondant icing

Two chocolate buttons

4 fan-shaped ice-cream wafers

A tub of ice cream

The pointy end of an ice-cream cone

Some colourful pouring sauce

HERE'S WHAT TO DO:

1 Wash your hands

2 Using green fondant icing, roll out a long 'sausage' shape and coil it up to make the tail. Shape four legs as shown and two goggly eyes. Use the chocolate buttons to make the eyes more realistic

3 Arrange two fan-shaped wafers together on a plate in a semi-circle

4 Place a large scoop of ice cream on top

5 Take the other two wafers and lay them on the ice cream in a semi-circle

6 Press down gently to make a 'sandwich', smooth off the edges then stand upright on your plate (see photo)

7 Fill the cone with ice cream and press on to form a 'head'

8 Push on the tail, legs and eyes

9 Drench with lots of colourful pouring sauce

10 Eat – quickly!

YUM!

Can't wait for the next book
in the series?
Here's a sneak preview of

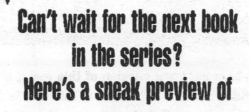

1. Home and Away

'And of course there will be – NO HOMEWORK!'

Everyone cheered as Mr Miller's face changed from super stern to super happy.

'That does NOT mean term has ended this minute,' bawled Mr Miller over the noise of pupils jumping about. 'Paul Parnell – Stewart Staines – sit DOWN! There's still lots of work to do.'

Everyone groaned loudly, and Mr Miller wished – not for the first time – that schools were still as they'd been in his grandparents' youth. He sighed, imagining rows of tidy, obedient, *quiet* children.

'I need someone to tidy the stationery cupboard,' said their teacher. 'No, not you, Vikki – I don't want pink bows round everything.'

They all laughed as Vikki Veale sulkily tossed her golden hair so that her dangly earrings shook. Mr Miller opened his mouth, then decided he really didn't care if she broke the school rules on jewellery on the last day.

Max Murphy and his best mate Jake Ramsbottom got the job of tidying the cupboard.

Max was really happy too. It was nearly the Easter holidays and, for once, he was *not* travelling abroad to meet his parents and go animal watching in some remote part of the world.

Jake thumped him on the back. 'Tomorrow,' he said, hurling books into piles so that Max could put them neatly on the shelves, 'we start on *Arctic*

Adventure!' It was their new computer game, which Max had bought with his saved-up pocket money. 'You can't spend a lot in the middle of the jungle,' he had explained to Jake, 'so it just mounts up.'

'You can bring the crisps,' said Max. He shuffled the geography books together and thought with glee that he wouldn't need to know ANYTHING about far-off places this holiday. The furthest he was going was to the shops to buy something really special for his twin sister Molly for Easter.

'You bet I will,' said Jake. 'I don't want to eat cornflake sandwiches with chilli sauce *ever* again!' When his parents were away, Max and his twin sister Molly lived with their Uncle Herbert. Jake and the twins dreaded Uncle Herbert's cooking. The last time Jake had been round, Herbert had served up vanilla-and-fish-paste ice cream. Poor Jake would never forget the experience. In fact, he'd eaten the ice cream a month ago, and he could *still* taste it!

120

Unfortunately, Stewart Staines was listening in.

'Cornflake sandwiches? Chilli sauce?' he sneered, swaggering over to lean on Jake's desk. 'Are you some kind of freak?'

'Nothing to do with you,' muttered Jake, walking away from the class bully.

'Leave him alone, Brain Strain!' said Max. 'How come you always believe everything we say? How thick is that?'

Stewart edged away. He'd tried getting the better of Max before, and hadn't won.

But it didn't matter what Stewart Staines said. There was a whole fortnight's holiday ahead of them, two weeks free of Brain Strain, his sidekick Paul Parnell and everyone else who annoyed them. *And*, Max thought thankfully, *I'll be at home!*

When the bell went, they left the cupboard half tidied and rushed out of the classroom, yelling at the tops of their voices.

'So, first we play *Arctic Adventure*, and second we play *Arctic Adventure* . . .'

'Then I've got to go shopping,' said Max, happily.

'More crisps,' agreed Jake.

'No,' said Max. 'I want to get a really cool Easter present for Molly. You know how she helps me when I change into animals? I'd be completely sunk if she didn't get my clothes to me when I change back.' Though he remembered with a grimace the time when Molly had brought him a *dress*. It wasn't just any dress: it was the frilly flowery one that Auntie Julie had given her last Christmas – even Molly hated it.

'Easter egg,' said Jake promptly, kicking a stone as they crossed the playground. It slammed into the fence with a satisfying ringing sound. He was never quite sure whether to believe Max's stories about his animal transformations. He'd never seen it happen

122

yet. But if the Murphy twins were going to be around all the Easter holidays, there was a good chance he might be there this time. He'd hate to think his best mate had been winding him up.

'She's not too keen on Easter eggs,' said Max. 'Well, not the usual ones with bows on.'

'Choccy football,' said Jake.

'Maybe,' said Max. 'Or a real football,' he said thoughtfully. 'The one she practises with is wearing out.' But maybe even that wouldn't be good enough. He'd have to scour the shops tomorrow to find something *really* special for his twin.

There was a noise like an express train going through a tunnel. Molly waved frantically to them and tore over, dragging their friend Samreen with her.

'It's the holidays!' she shrieked. 'And we're not going anywhere!'

Samreen grinned. Only the Murphy twins would

be glad they weren't going abroad for their holidays.

'Computer games every day!' said Max dreamily.

'*Football* every day!' said Molly. 'You want to try it – get off your bottom and have a bit of exercise. Mum and Dad won't let you stay in all day in front of a computer screen.'

'Want a bet?' said Max. Maybe he wouldn't bother to get her a present after all, if all he got were insults!

Squabbling happily, they walked home.

Molly got there first, as usual. She thrust her way through the door, letting it slam behind her, practically in Max's face.

'Mum! Dad! Guess what? Samreen's coming

with me to play football. We've signed up for the holiday course – you don't mind paying do you? It's Mondays, Wednesdays and Fridays, at the *stadium*! We get coaching from all the top people there . . .'

Max threw his schoolbag on the floor and grinned at his parents. 'We're gonna beat the world record and win more points than anyone *ever*!' he said. 'I'm gonna have a quick practise tonight so Jake doesn't get ahead of me, so if it's OK I'll go up and switch on the computer now . . .'

'Hey, wait a bit!' laughed Mrs Murphy, pulling herself free from Molly's strangling hug. 'That all sounds wonderful, but can you pack it all into a couple of days? The thing is . . .' She turned with shining eyes to her husband. 'We've got some news.'

Max's heart thumped right down into his dirty trainers. He looked at Molly. Her big grin was already sliding downwards. They didn't have to wait for their parents to come up with the amazing news. They knew what it was going to be.

'A once-in-a-lifetime opportunity,' said Manfred Murphy, his quiet smile showing how much he wanted this.

Mrs Murphy's hair seemed even more wild and bushy than usual, as if it was joining in her excitement. 'You remember that earthquake in the Arctic, that was on the news a couple of weeks ago?'

'Yeah,' muttered Max, kicking his bag into a corner. He could feel a disappointed lump in his throat that wouldn't go away.

'They want us to go and study the after-effects on the wildlife in the area,' enthused his father.

'And, of course, we want you both to come with us!' said his mother excitedly.

'Oh,' said Molly. 'Will we get to see polar bears?'

'Maybe,' her mum answered.

'Can't we stay with Uncle Herbert?' said Max, desperately.

'I'm sorry, darling,' said Mrs Murphy, 'but your uncle's off on a trip of his own this time. Besides, it will do you so much good. Think of what you'll see – arctic foxes, seals ...'

'P-penguins,' sniffed Max, fighting the lump in his throat.

'They're only found at the South Pole, Max,' exclaimed his dad. 'If you don't know a simple fact like that then you're definitely coming with us, and that's final!'